THIS WALKER BOOK BELONGS TO:

Daniel

For Ralph

First published 2004 by Walker Books Ltd
87 Vauxhall Walk, London SE11 5HJ

This edition produced 2008 for Bookstart

10 9 8 7 6 5 4 3 2 1

© 2004 Petr Horáček

The right of Petr Horáček to be identified as author/illustrator
of this work has been asserted by him in accordance
with the Copyright, Designs and Patents Act 1988

This book has been typeset in Barmeno

Printed in China

British Library Cataloguing in Publication Data:
a catalogue record for this book is available from the British Library

ISBN 978-1-4063-1633-9

www.walkerbooks.co.uk

WALKER BOOKS
AND SUBSIDIARIES
LONDON · BOSTON · SYDNEY · AUCKLAND

A New House
for Mouse

Petr Horáček

One day a little mouse looked out of the tiny
hole where she lived and saw a huge apple.

"Goodness me," said Little Mouse. "I would
like that apple to eat. I must bring it inside."

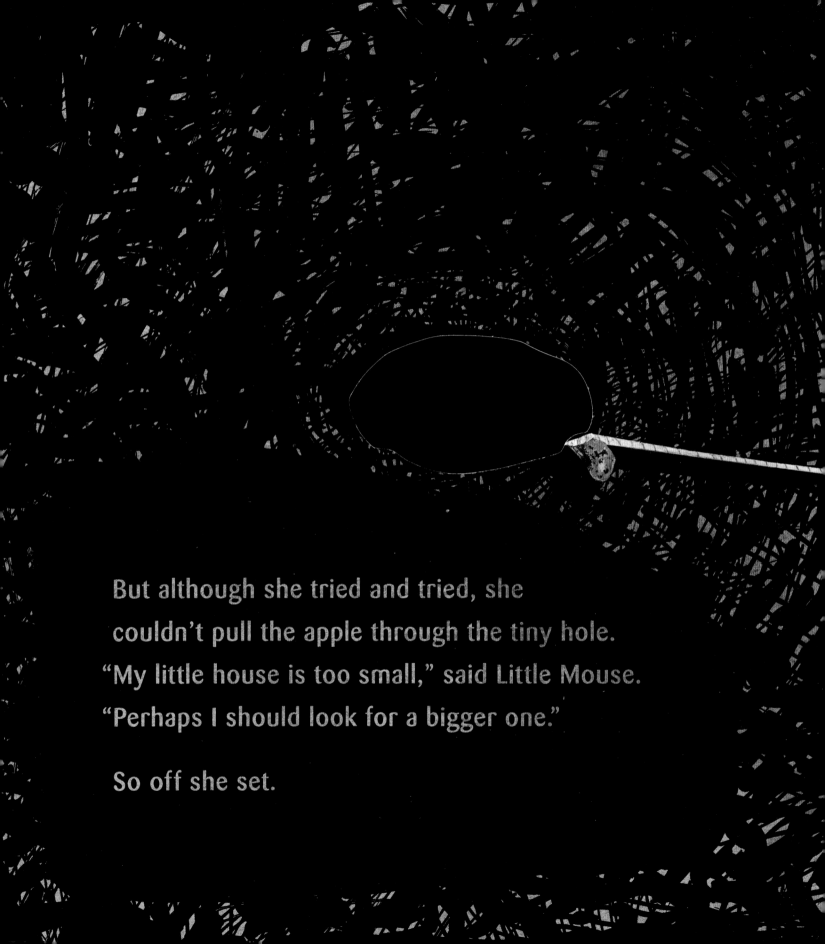

But although she tried and tried, she
couldn't pull the apple through the tiny hole.
"My little house is too small," said Little Mouse.
"Perhaps I should look for a bigger one."

So off she set.

"Looking for a new house
   makes you hungry," said Little Mouse
as she took a few bites of the juicy apple. Then she
spotted a hole that was just a little bigger than hers.
"This looks just right," she said as she peered inside.

"Hello, Mole," she
said. "I need a bigger
house for me and my apple.
Can I live here with you?"
"I'm sorry," mumbled Mole,
"but my home is too full
of books and I don't think
there's room for both of us."
"Perhaps not," said Little Mouse,
"I'll keep looking."

As she wandered, Little Mouse felt hungry.
"I'll just have a nibble," she said to herself.
Then she spotted a hole that was just a little bigger
than Mole's. "That will be perfect," she said.

She peered inside.

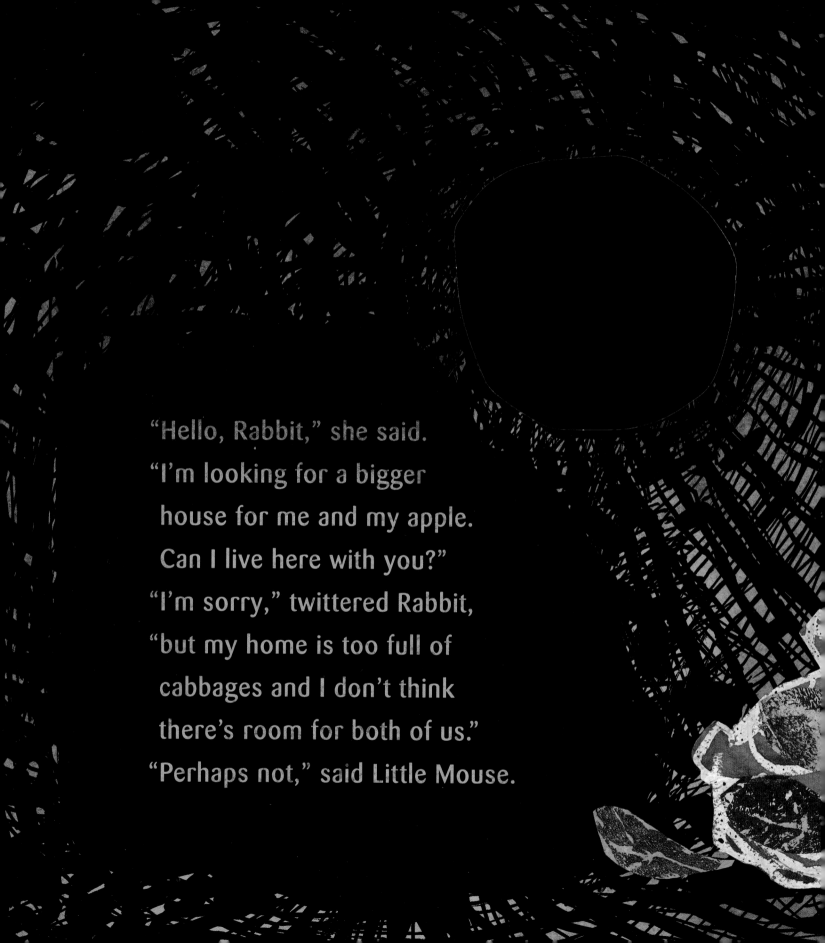

"Hello, Rabbit," she said.
"I'm looking for a bigger
house for me and my apple.
Can I live here with you?"
"I'm sorry," twittered Rabbit,
"but my home is too full of
cabbages and I don't think
there's room for both of us."
"Perhaps not," said Little Mouse.

She set off again, but she was still hungry,
so she nibbled on the apple as she went. Then she
spotted another hole that was just a little bigger than
Rabbit's. "That will be just right," she said.

She peered inside.

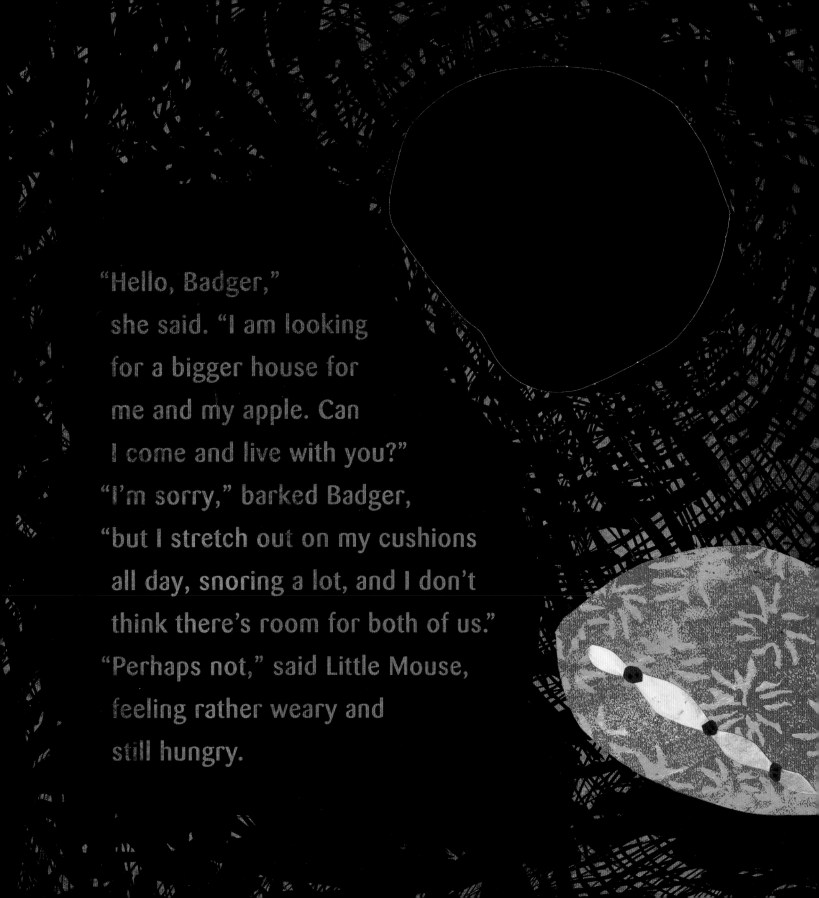

"Hello, Badger,"
she said. "I am looking
for a bigger house for
me and my apple. Can
I come and live with you?"
"I'm sorry," barked Badger,
"but I stretch out on my cushions
all day, snoring a lot, and I don't
think there's room for both of us."
"Perhaps not," said Little Mouse,
feeling rather weary and
still hungry.

That evening she came across an enormous hole. This must be big enough for me and my apple, she thought.

"Hello! Is anybody there?" she shouted.

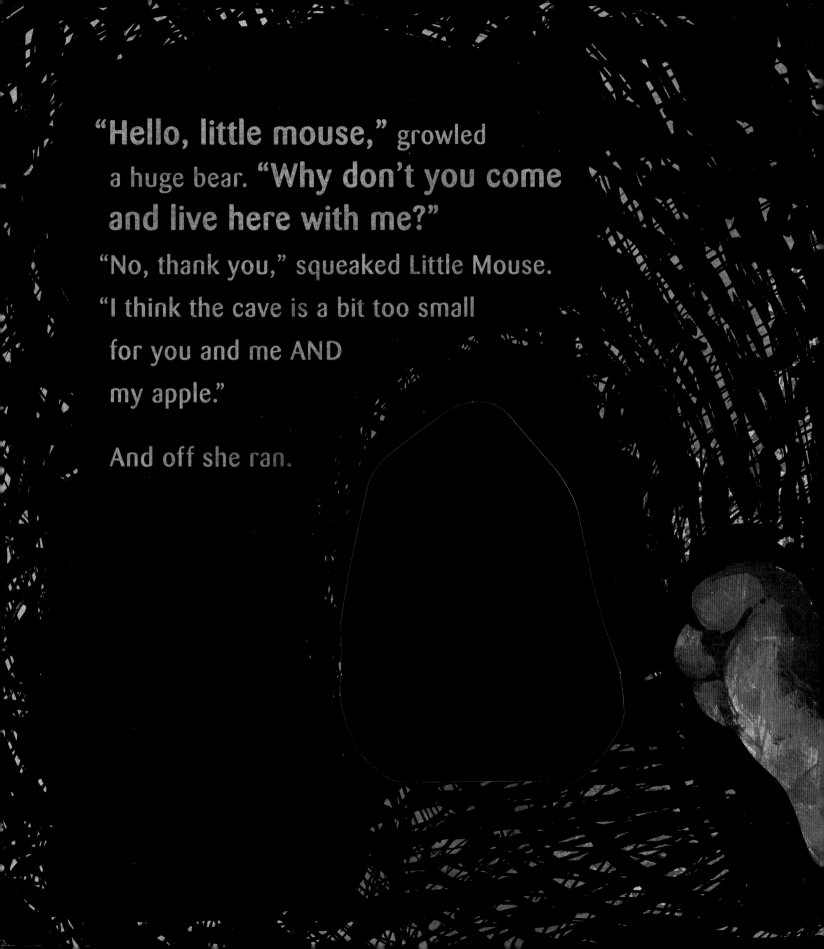

"Hello, little mouse," growled a huge bear. "Why don't you come and live here with me?"

"No, thank you," squeaked Little Mouse. "I think the cave is a bit too small

for you and me AND

my apple."

And off she ran.

Hello, little mouse," growled
a huge bear. **"Why don't you come
and live here with me?"**

No, thank you," squeaked Little Mouse.

I think the cave is a bit too small

for you and me AND

my apple."

And off she ran.

Little Mouse was tired now,
but pulling the apple seemed easier.
Suddenly she saw a tiny hole. "That
looks perfect," she squeaked.
"I wonder who lives here…"

She peered inside.

There was no one
at home. Little Mouse
went right in and pulled
her apple behind her.

It fitted perfectly.

"I knew I would find somewhere
just right for both me and my apple,"
she said, and she climbed into her
own bed and fell fast asleep.